Skating
Dreams
Champion's Luck

Read all the *Skating Dreams* books!

#1: *The Turning Point*

#2: *Staying Balanced*

#3: *Skating Backward*

#4: *Champion's Luck*

Coming soon:

#5: *The Winning Edge*

Skating Dreams

Champion's Luck

By Nola Thacker

Hyperion Paperbacks for Children

New York

Printed in the United States of America
First Edition
1 3 5 7 9 10 8 6 4 2
This book is set in 12.5-point Life.
ISBN: 0-7868-1379-2
Visit www.skatingdreams.com

I

∽

"Annie!" Lauren Wing shouted. "Are you all right?" She raced across the ice, her heart pounding. One minute, Annie McGrath was doing a basic crossover as carefully as if she had just started learning to ice skate. The next minute, she had crashed to the ice.

Danielle Kurowicki, who'd stopped to reknot her laces, straightened up when she heard Lauren shout. Her hands flew to her chest. She started forward, forgetting the flapping lace, and almost fell herself.

By now, Lauren had reached Annie. Annie's cheeks flamed red, making her freckles stand out. Lauren couldn't tell if Annie was

1

embarrassed or angry, the usual causes of Annie's blushes and what she called her "freckle attacks."

Everyone else on the ice kept skating calmly, as if a kid falling were no big deal.

It wasn't, Lauren thought. Not usually.

But the last time Annie had fallen, she'd fallen hard—so hard that she hadn't been able to even think about skating for over a month. She'd had to struggle to get back on the ice. Now Annie was working harder than Lauren had ever seen her work to try to get ready for Regional Championships.

But no one knew if she'd be ready in time.

"Annie! Where does it hurt? Don't move! Sit still!" Danielle skated over to her friends. Usually her dramatics were exaggerated, but not now. Lauren could tell that Danielle was freaked out by Annie's tumble.

Annie finally spoke. She took a deep breath and said, "I just fell. I'm fine. Don't worry about it, okay?" In spite of Danielle's worried exclamation, Annie got to her feet.

Lauren glanced over toward Coach Knudson,

who was teaching a very young beginners' class at the far end of the rink. She had stopped her class and was watching the three girls.

Lauren waved to show that everything was all right.

Coach Knudson's shoulder's relaxed and she nodded and smiled back before returning to her class.

Danielle was helping Annie to her feet. She kept a tight grip on Annie's arm and said, "You're sure? Absolutely, one-thousand percent sure?"

"Danielle," Annie said through clenched teeth. "Please let go of my arm."

Danielle let go. She stepped back to a safe distance. Annie had a quick temper and Danielle could tell when she was about to lose it.

Annie took a few more deep breaths. The red left her face. She gave Lauren and Danielle a sheepish smile. "Sorry, guys," she said. "It's just, well, I'm okay, okay? If I hurt myself when I fall, I promise I'll yell. Really loudly. But until then, treat me like . . . me. A skater."

Once again Danielle's hands went to her chest. She laced her fingers and pressed her hands over her heart and made an elegant bow. "As you wish," she said grandly.

"Thanks," said Annie. "Now, are we going to practice, or what?"

"No hands," Danielle said promptly. That meant they would play Follow the Leader but that all moves had to be done without using their hands. It was their goofy version of a balance drill.

"No hands, no problem," said Annie promptly. Danielle took off. Annie burned up the ice right behind her.

Lauren watched them for a moment. The ice was her favorite place to be, and having Annie back made being there even nicer. Lauren could remember all too clearly how depressed Annie had been when she was injured. But now she was determined to be ready for Regionals. With hard work, she had a chance.

With hard work *and* friends and luck, Lauren thought, watching as Annie drew alongside Danielle. Danielle said something and made a dramatic gesture. Annie laughed and shook her head. The two took off again.

Danielle had skated badly at recent events. In contrast to Annie and Lauren, she didn't seem focused. Danielle had not placed in a previous competition and her chances of going to Regionals were squashed. But last week, Coach Knudson told Danielle that a girl broke her ankle and couldn't compete. Danielle had a second chance! She was going to Regionals with Lauren and Annie.

Regionals were a huge event. Placing at the Regionals was the first step on the way to the Eastern Sectionals, where winning led in turn to the Novice National Championships.

"Hey! Are you going to stand there all day, or are you going to practice?" Danielle called.

"Coming," Lauren said. She pushed off, and glided across the ice to join her friends, leaving the thoughts of the hard times behind, at least for a little while.

2

"We made it!" Lacey Wing, age eight, burst through the kitchen door like the high-speed star wing of the soccer team that she was. "I got an assist. Our goalie, Jacie, made this incredible save. *Boom!* Punched it right over the top of the goal!"

"We won! We won! We won!" Five-year-old Lisa danced into the kitchen behind her dirt-and-grass-stained sister. "I want to be a goalie when I grow up, and catch the ball."

"You won? Congratulations!" Lauren had just gotten home from practice at the rink. She hadn't been able to go to Lacey's game. But she knew how important winning that game had been to Lacey. Lacey was as passionate about soccer as Lauren was about skating.

"If we win two more games, we'll qualify for the Western State Division Championship," Lacey went on.

"If you don't get cleaned up and start helping us get dinner on the table before your mother and Bryan get home, you're going to qualify for double dish duty," said Mr. Wing. But he was smiling.

"Hey! We won. Doesn't that count for anything?" Lacey said.

"It counts. So do your other responsibilities," Mr. Wing answered.

Lacey's eyes met Lauren's. She rolled her eyes and Lauren smiled. Their father was in what Lacey called his Robo-Pop mold: saying strict things because he couldn't help himself, even though he knew that Lacey wouldn't goof off and not do her part.

"Winning isn't everything," Lacey said. She walked to the door, turned, and wrinkled her nose. "It's the ONLY thing!" With a shout of triumphant laughter, she raced out of the kitchen and up the stairs. A few minutes later, a bathroom door slammed and the walls shook with the sound of running water and Lacey's singing loud and off-key as she showered.

"Wash your hands," Mr. Wing said, lifting Lisa up so she could reach the sink. When she'd finished, he set her down and Lauren handed Lisa the spoons to put out. The spoons and napkins were Lisa's job at every meal, setting them out and picking them up.

"How was practice?" her father asked as he began to unpack the bag he had brought from the family restaurant. Lauren's nose twitched. "Cashew vegetables?" she asked.

He nodded. "Lacey's favorite, to celebrate winning," he said.

"I'm sorry I missed the game," Lauren said. "But I can't miss a single practice. Not with Regionals so close and . . . and all." She wondered if her father had noticed her hesitation.

But he only nodded, and began taking serving dishes from the pantry.

Lauren began to fill glasses with water. She had almost said, "I can't afford to miss a single practice. Not with Regionals so close and no coach."

Almost. Not because she'd meant to say anything. She knew her parents felt bad about the fact that the Wing family didn't have any extra money right now to pay for expensive coaching for Lauren's figure skating.

Lauren had accepted it. She really had. She knew it wasn't forever. She knew that the hard times would get better and she'd get to work with Coach Perry again.

But accepting it didn't mean not thinking about it. Lauren couldn't help thinking about it, often. Even with the help of her friends, and all the practice in the world, she didn't see how she could do her absolute, 100-percent best at Regionals without a coach.

She wasn't an experienced enough skater to know when she was making mistakes, possibly even practicing them, maybe adding them to her routine. She needed a coach to tell her when a jump wasn't working, when she was traveling during a spin, and a hundred other things.

The only thing she didn't need a coach for

was to make Lauren give 100-percent effort at every practice. Lauren always worked her hardest at skating, but that was because it didn't feel like work. For her, it was what she loved doing most in the world.

The door opened again. This time it was Lauren's mother and her older brother, Bryan. By the smile on Mrs. Wing's face, Lauren knew she had heard the good news about Lacey's soccer game.

"Just in time for dinner," Mr. Wing said. "Bryan . . ."

"I'm going," Bryan said, rolling his eyes and looking so much like Lacey had earlier that Lauren had to laugh. "I'll wash my hands and be right down."

"Me, too," said Mrs. Wing, smiling at her husband.

A few minutes later, as he placed the last dish in the center of the table and sat down, Mr. Wing said, "You know, sometimes I feel as if we are all going in a thousand directions at once. Mom at the bookstore, me at the restaurant, Bryan working at the The Penalty Box restaurant and playing hockey, Lauren practicing so hard, Lacey playing soccer—where *is* Lacey?"

As if on cue, Lacey raced in and slid into her chair. "Here," she said. She beamed at everyone. "Did I tell you how we won the game?"

"Tell us all over again," said Lisa happily.

"Don't worry," said Bryan. "She will."

"We killed them," Lacey said. "Our goalie made a great save and I got an assist. Our coach said I was definitely MVP material. . . ."

Coach, Lauren thought, and wondered what Coach Perry was doing. Only a few months before, she'd been on top of the world, just like Lacey. That was when nationally famous coach Eve Perry had offered to work with Lauren. With that offer had come a membership in the new skating rink, Silver Springs Ice Rink in Saratoga Springs. Lauren had had to get up before dawn four mornings a week to meet Coach Perry there for her lesson before school—the only time that both Coach Perry and the ice were available. She'd had to rearrange her schedule and see even less of her family and of her best skating buddies, Danielle

11

and Annie, and of her best friend at school, Rebecca.

It had been hard. But it had been worth it. It had been a big, shining step on the way to Lauren's most secret dream of skating someday in the Olympics.

But then, just like that, the dream had become almost a mockery. Money worries had swamped her family. In addition to working as a bookkeeper at the family restaurant, her mother had gotten a part-time job at a local bookstore. And Lauren had had to give up her skating lessons.

No other way. She was on her own.

But she wouldn't quit. Lauren didn't have Annie's quick temper but she had more than her share of stubbornness. Unconsciously she raised her chin in defiance—and met her father's eyes. He smiled as if he could read her thoughts.

But if he could read her thoughts, why was he smiling?

3

Now her mother and father were smiling at each other. Lacey, who had finished her soccer victory story, began to pick all the cashews out of the stir-fried cashew vegetables and crunch them noisily.

Usually, this would have earned a quick "You know better than that, young lady," from her mother or father.

But not now.

Lacey noticed it, too. She stopped crunching and stared at her parents.

"What?" she said. Then, her voice rising, "You're not about to tell us we're going to get a new baby brother or sister, are you?"

"No," said Mrs. Wing, her eyes crinkling in amusement.

"It's a different kind of good news," Mr. Wing said.

"What? What're you guys talking about?" asked Bryan, looking confused. He clearly had been paying more attention to his plate than his parents.

Now both of her parents were staring at Lauren. And they were smiling big, dumb grins.

"What?" Lauren asked. "What's the good news?" In spite of herself, one hand went to her chest in a dramatic, Danielle-like motion. But when Danielle dramatically pressed her hands against her heart, did her heart feel as if it might jump out of her chest, as Lauren's did now?

There was only one piece of good news worth hearing, for Lauren. Only one sentence her parents could say that would deserve the word "good."

"If the hard times aren't over," her father said, "they're not as hard."

Her mother nodded. "I'm going to keep working at the bookstore, but fewer hours. I enjoy working there, and the extra money is nice."

Lauren wasn't sure when she stopped breathing, but it might have been at that moment. "My lessons," she managed to say.

Her mother nodded, delight filling her face. "We can afford your lessons again. Three a week, for now. We'll add to that when we can."

Lauren let out a shriek. She couldn't help herself.

Bryan clapped his hands over his ears. "Ouch!" he complained. "I think you just went sonar."

"Sonar?" asked Lacey.

"She screamed so high, bats could hear her," Bryan explained.

But Lauren paid no attention to her brother's teasing. She jumped up and ran around the table to hug first her mother and then her father.

"I guess this means you want to start lessons again," her father said.

"When? When can I start?" Lauren demanded.

"Mondays, Wednesdays, and Fridays," her

father said. "Starting this Monday. How does that sound?"

"It'll do," said Lauren, her face almost cracking apart she was smiling so hard. "It'll do just fine!"

"That is so great. Incredibly, perfectly excellent," Rebecca Meyers said.

Lauren had taken the phone into the bedroom she shared with Lisa and Lacey. Lisa was having her bath. Lacey was helping with after-dinner cleanup, and still talking soccer.

Lauren laughed at how dramatic Rebecca sounded. "You sound like Danielle," Lauren teased.

Of course, Rebecca was nothing like Danielle. She and Lauren had been best buddies since first grade. Jealous rivalry had brought them together, literally, in a playground fight over Randy Bishop, a boy who to that day tried to impress his classmates with his ability to do gross tricks, like turning his eyelids inside out. In first grade it had been a winning talent. Now, Rebecca and Lauren had moved on from Randy.

But they had remained best friends, as different as two best friends could be.

For one thing, Rebecca's favorite ice was in cubes, in the freezer. She couldn't understand Lauren's passion for figure skating, but she was always ready to cheer her on.

And if Lauren didn't understand Rebecca's scientific view of the world, she admired her for it. Lauren thought Rebecca might be one of the smartest people she knew. And she knew that Rebecca was one of the kindest. Rebecca was an only child—if you didn't count the seven cats and two dachshunds that lived at her house. She and her parents were always rescuing stray animals, and the cats were those for which they had not been able to find homes.

It had been Rebecca who had rescued Lutz as a starving, gray scrap of a kitten, and given him to Lauren.

"So now you can get ready for Regionals big time," Rebecca said.

"You better believe it. I'm going to work soooo hard. Coach Perry will never know I've been away," Lauren said.

"You can do it," Rebecca agreed.

"I hope you're right," Lauren said, her heart overflowing with happiness. She wanted to be out on the ice, right now.

But right now, she had homework to do, and it was time for Lisa to go to bed. Lauren could hear her youngest sister in the hall.

Lauren sighed, a sigh of happiness and impatience. "Gotta go," she said.

She hung up the phone. She'd tell Danielle and Annie tomorrow at practice.

She'd squeeze in all the extra practice she could between now and her first return lesson with Coach Perry next week. It was a variation on the old joke: Can you tell me how to get to Carnegie Hall?

Practice, practice, practice.

How did you get to the Olympics?

Lauren smiled and fell back across her bed, her eyes dreamy.

"Practice," she whispered. "Practice, practice, practice."

4

"Why are you smiling like that?" asked
Danielle.

"Well . . ." Lauren said.

She paused, still a little giddy with joy. She
was back, really back. With Coach Perry, she
would have a chance at winning, at truly being
the best.

Annie came hustling up, breathless. "Hey,"
she said. "Listen. I want you guys to come over
to my house Friday night. We'll have a sleepover."

"I can't," said Lauren, smiling more hugely
than ever.

Annie looked at her strangely. "Okay," she

said. "But why does that make you so happy? You don't like sleepovers? You don't like coming to my house?"

"I have to get up extra early to practice on Saturday morning. And I want to get in a practice in the afternoon, too," Lauren said. "If I sleep over, I might be too tired."

"Too tired to skate? You? Never," said Danielle. "Not in about ten million years."

Staring hard at Lauren, Annie sat down and began removing her skate guards. "Something happened," she stated. She stood up. "What?"

"You're right!" Danielle peered at Lauren. "If you smiled any harder, you'd look like one of those little smiley-face buttons."

When Lauren had seen Rebecca at school, Rebecca's high-five and cheerful congratulations had felt very satisfying.

But Lauren was going to enjoy breaking the news to Annie and Danielle even more. She took a deep breath and said, "My parents . . . Coach Perry . . ." She didn't get to finish.

Danielle leaped up in the air, gaining height she hadn't demonstrated in a jump for a long time. "NO WAY!" she shouted. "INSANE! FABULOUS FOREVER MAD PERFECT!"

People turned to stare, but Danielle didn't care. Her round face was split with a smile almost as wide as Lauren's and her halo of blond curls bobbed as she pumped both fists in the air.

Annie threw both arms around Lauren, making the air go out of her with an "oof." "That is so, *so* great," she said. "Oh, Lauren! When do you start?"

"Lessons begin this Monday morning," Lauren said. She paused to savor the words. "This Monday morning," she repeated. "So you see, I have to get in all the practice I can. I don't want to let Coach Perry down."

"You're not coming to my game?" Lacey's face fell.

Lauren dropped her skate bag on the ground. "Oh, Lacey, I can't. I have to practice," she said.

"But you practiced this morning. Right after breakfast," Lacey said. "If you practice too much, you'll lose your edge."

"Maybe in soccer, but not in figure skating," Lauren said. "You can never practice too much. I'm going for perfection here."

"It's only an hour," Lacey said.

"Is it one of the big games?" Lauren said, wavering at the look on her middle sister's face.

Slowly, Lacey shook her head. "Not exactly," she said. "We don't have to win this one. I mean, they're not in our division. It's for practice."

"See? You're practicing, too," Lauren said.

Lacey wheeled her bicycle into the garage next to where Lauren stood by her own bike. "I guess," she said. She made a face. "But you'll come to our playoff game, won't you?"

"I wouldn't miss it," Lauren said promptly.

"Promise?"

"Cross my heart and hope to die," Lauren promised.

Lacey rolled her eyes.

"You know, rolling your eyes like that is bad

for your eyesight," Lauren said. "It could ruin your soccer game."

Lacey rolled her eyes again. "Uh-huh. I've got to go get suited up for the game."

"Good luck," said Lauren.

"Thanks," said Lacey.

"And I want to hear all about it tonight," Lauren added.

"You will," Lacey said matter-of-factly.

Lauren watched her sister bound into the house and felt a pang of guilt. But she shook it off. If you wanted to be a winner, you had to set priorities. And right now, her number-one priority was being perfect for her lesson on Monday morning.

She wheeled her bike out of the garage and swung her leg over it. The skate bag bumped against her back as she pedaled onto the sidewalk as if to say, "You're wasting time. Hurry."

Lauren picked up speed and felt the weariness in her legs. It was a good thing she hadn't gone to the sleepover at Annie's. She'd have been up most of the night, watching videos and sending e-mails to friends and a hundred other silly things.

She didn't have time to be silly now—not if she was going to be a winner.

Lauren woke up well before her father opened the door and whispered "Good morning!"

She felt almost as excited as the morning that now seemed so long ago when she'd gotten up to make the long drive to the new skating rink for her first session with Coach Perry. It felt good to be getting up in the darkness to get dressed in the bathroom where she'd put her clothes the night before. Her skate bag and school pack stood by the front door, waiting for her, just as before. And when Lauren reached the van, she found her father sitting in the driver's seat, sipping a cup of coffee. It was as if she'd never missed a morning in the routine.

I just hope that is how Coach Perry feels, she thought, as she slid into the seat and buckled her seat belt.

5

Lauren stepped out onto the ice at the Silver Springs rink and felt the cold rise around her legs. A thin layer of frosty vapor curled above clean, new ice smoothed by her father on the Zamboni machine. Far above, the top tiers of bleachers were in near darkness.

Lauren looked around and let out a sigh of pure happiness.

"Let's get started," said Coach Perry, as if Lauren had never been away.

Lauren turned to look at the tiny, imposing figure of her coach. As usual, she wore no gloves. Today, the only sign of her favorite color, a bright taxi yellow, was in the scarf around her neck. She wore a heavy Nordic sweater of silver gray and black legwarmers over black ski pants. Her fingernails were brilliant scarlet.

"Okay," said Lauren, smiling. She hadn't been able to stop smiling since her parents had told her the news.

Coach Perry smiled too. The smile warmed Lauren down to her ice-rink-cold toes. Coach Perry said, "First, a few times around to warm up, basic moves. Then we begin. At the beginning."

Lauren nodded. She pushed off and began to skate.

"So," Coach Perry said at the end of the lesson. "You have not failed to practice during your absence. Good."

This was high praise from Coach Perry. "No. I mean, yes, I've practiced. A lot." Lauren's smile wasn't as wide as when their session had begun. She was tired. Her brain ached from how hard she had been concentrating on doing each element exactly right. Coach Perry had, as usual, been a perfectionist. Lauren had repeated some moves not once or twice, but dozens and dozens of times.

Lauren bent forward, trying to catch her breath. Coach Perry tapped herself on the forehead and told Lauren, "I talk, you listen. Up here, you understand. This is good. But only when your body understands have I done my job."

Lauren's body understood one thing now at least—it was tired.

"Until Wednesday, then," Coach Perry said.

"Wednesday," Lauren repeated. She took a deep breath, sat down, and began to unlace her skates.

"Where's Danielle?" Lauren asked.

Annie shook her head. "Coach Knudson said Danielle called and said she had something she had to do at school."

"Too bad," Lauren said sincerely.

"Yeah," said Annie. "Well, it could have been worse—it could have been the dentist or something."

Lauren, Annie, and Danielle only allowed

school and doctor's appointments to cut into their time on the ice. And with Regionals coming closer day by day, getting in every single moment of practice was especially important.

"How'd it go this morning?" Annie asked.

They skated slowly, side by side as they talked. Lauren's legs felt heavy. How quickly she'd gotten out of the habit of having two sessions on ice in a single day!

Abruptly, Annie stopped. She veered and began to skate along the far side of the rink.

"Hey," Lauren complained, scrambling to keep up. "If we're going to play Follow the Leader, give me some warning."

"Incoming Erica, on your left," Annie hissed out of the corner of her mouth. She began to skate faster.

Lauren did the same. That was the only problem with a skating rink—it wasn't big enough to escape from Erica Claiborn. She glided up to them on long, graceful legs and an expression of smiling malice. With her dark hair and expensive skating outfits, she looked like a magazine advertisement for a figure skater.

But, as Annie was fond of saying, when they were handing out nice, Erica must have been in the bathroom admiring herself in the mirror. She seemed to live to pick on Annie, Danielle, and Lauren, particularly Lauren.

Today, however, Lauren wasn't Erica's special target. She pulled alongside and said, "Two busy little wanna-be winners, I see."

"Whatever," said Annie. Her freckles were starting to stand out.

Lauren bumped Annie's shoulder slightly to remind her to relax and not let Erica get to her.

Erica smiled. It was a judge-worthy smile, a perfect six—until you looked closely and saw the meanness in her pale blue eyes.

"But only two of the three stooges? Where's Danielle?"

Annie shrugged.

"Oh, that's right. She's at school," Erica said. "She finally got smart—or at least, a little smarter."

Lauren glanced at Annie to see if Annie had

any idea what Erica was talking about. Annie shook her head slightly. Annie and Lauren went to the same school, where Annie was a year ahead of Lauren. But Danielle went to Pine Creek Academy, the private school that Erica attended, so Annie, like Lauren, hadn't seen Danielle all day.

Lauren couldn't help it. She asked, "What are you talking about, Erica?"

"She didn't tell you? I thought you were all *such* good friends." Erica shook her head. "Danielle signed up to try out for the school play. They're going to do *The Wizard of Oz*. Isn't that sweet?" Erica laughed.

"Danielle wouldn't skip skating for a play," Annie said firmly.

"She's obviously seen the truth—that she'll never make it as a skater. At least one of you has some brains," Erica said. "I just hope Danielle doesn't want the starring role. She's no Dorothy. She should stick to roles that are better suited to her—like the Scarecrow."

"I guess you already have the Wicked Witch nailed down. Right, Erica?" Lauren said.

Erica hadn't expected that. Lauren usually kept quiet around Erica, when she couldn't avoid talking to her at all. Spots of red color bloomed on Erica's cheeks.

"I do not!" Erica almost shouted.

"Well, keep practicing," Annie joined in. "You're *perfect* for the part."

Erica spun in a spray of ice and skated furiously away.

Annie raised her eyebrows at Lauren. "Good one, Lauren. Erica the Wicked Witch."

"Whatever," Lauren said. "Annie—you don't think it's true, do you? You don't think Danielle blew off skating for a school play?"

"No! How could she?" Annie said.

"Maybe . . . maybe she's just checking it out, you know?" Lauren said. "I mean, Danielle knows she can't practice skating *and* rehearse for a play at the same time."

"Danielle would never give up skating," Annie said. She paused. "But she *does* like drama. She's talked about being an actor. . . ." Annie's voice trailed off.

"Center stage for center ice?" Lauren said.

She didn't like the sound of it. She didn't like the idea of Danielle not being there. Not at all.

Great, she thought. Just when life got back to normal, it got all weird again.

6

"Hey! Watch it!" Rebecca grabbed her red book bag and glared at Randy Bishop as he bumped into her shoulder on his way up the front steps of the school, tripping over Rebecca's bag.

Randy collided dramatically with a brick column by the front door. He staggered back, waving his arms.

Rebecca and Lauren both leaped toward him. Rebecca got there first, just as Randy dropped to his knees and fell forward—face first.

Other kids were turning to stare. Randy hadn't moved.

"Randy?" Rebecca said, her voice going up in disbelief.

More kids were looking in their direction.

Randy still didn't move.

"Randy!" Rebecca knelt beside him and shook his shoulder.

He remained motionless.

"I think you killed him," offered David Barker, one of Randy's buddies. Now people had started to gather around them.

"I'm sure he's okay," Lauren said. This was a totally embarrassing moment. "Get up, Randy," she ordered.

"I don't think he's dead," someone else said. "But he looks like you knocked him out."

"Probably a concussion," David said. He was a short kid with a wide grin and a reputation for being smart.

Lauren felt a twinge of uneasiness. She glanced at Rebecca.

But Rebecca had leaned back on her heels and was inspecting Randy's motionless body through narrowed eyes. Suddenly, she reached out and pinched Randy on the back of the neck—hard.

Randy rolled over with a screech. "OWWW! What're you doing? That hurt!"

David began to laugh.

Looking completely disgusted, Rebecca got to her feet. Randy got up too, rubbing his neck. "I think I'm bruised," he said. "Damaged."

"Damaged is a good word for you," Rebecca said.

"Good one, Randy," said David. He punched Randy on the shoulder.

"Stupid," said Rebecca.

"I scared you. Admit it," Randy said, smirking.

Now other people had begun to laugh.

"Oh, *grow up*," Rebecca said. "Let's go, Lauren."

Randy and David and his buddies were still laughing and hooting as Rebecca led the way into the building.

"I can't believe I ever thought he was cute," Rebecca said, stalking down the hall toward her locker.

"Well, we *were* in first grade," Lauren reminded her.

"Only a first grader could like Randy—then or now," Rebecca retorted.

"At least you pinched him good and hard. How did you know he was faking it?" Lauren asked.

"Scientific deduction," Rebecca said. "He didn't hit his head when he ran into the post. And I saw him catch himself with his arms right before he flattened out on the ground. If he'd been knocked out, he wouldn't have fallen so carefully."

"You sound like a detective," Lauren said.

"Good scientists are good detectives," said Rebecca.

From out of nowhere, Annie appeared. "It's true," she said, without even saying hello. "Can you believe Danielle would do something like that?"

"Hi, Annie," Rebecca said.

"She's crazy. She's lost her mind," Annie went on.

"Everyone's crazy today," Rebecca remarked. "What're you talking about, Annie?"

"Danielle!" Annie said. She turned to Lauren. "You haven't told Rebecca what Danielle did?"

"I—" Lauren began.

"She's trying out for the lead role in her school play. *The Wizard of Oz!*" Annie said.

"She is?" gasped Lauren.

"Did you talk to Danielle last night, Lauren?" Annie asked.

Lauren shook her head. "Homework. Then I went to bed early."

The real truth was that she had almost fallen asleep over her homework. She'd had to struggle to stay awake long enough to finish it. She'd been even more tired from her first full day back on the ice than she'd realized.

"Danielle could get the part. What's so bad about that? She'd be a great actor," said Rebecca.

"She's a skater, not an actor!" said Annie, outraged.

That made both Lauren and Rebecca laugh. After a moment, Annie grinned. "Okay, so Danielle has dramatic talent."

"No kidding," Lauren said.

"But she should save it for the ice," Annie said.

"There are other things in life besides skating," Rebecca said.

A moment of shocked silence followed. Annie and Lauren both stared at Rebecca as if she had suddenly arrived from another planet.

"There are," Rebecca insisted.

Just then, the bell rang. With a frown at Rebecca, Annie said, "We can talk about this later." To Lauren she said, "See you this afternoon at practice." Then she turned and disappeared down the hall.

As Rebecca and Lauren walked to class, Rebecca looked at Lauren. There *is* more to life than skating, you know."

"I know," said Lauren. "But I can't imagine life without it." She wasn't smiling at all.

Rebecca's smile faded. She patted Lauren's arm. "I know," she said. "I know."

Lauren closed her book with a satisfying snap.

Lutz, who'd come into the kitchen in hopes of a kitty treat and settled on a chair to wait, said, "Mrrow?" in a hopeful voice.

"Done," said Lauren. "Finished. This kitchen is officially a homework-done zone."

"Mrra," Lutz said. Lauren knew that he was saying he might starve if she didn't give him a kitty treat. Now.

Lauren reached over and pulled him onto her lap. He was purring already and he immediately began to purr even more loudly. She pressed her face to his soft fur. "There's more to life than kitty treats, Lutz," she told him.

He purred on, his eyes narrowing into slits. "Sure there is," she said, as if he were arguing with her. "Chasing mice and leaves and toys. Getting petted. Hiding in paper bags when the groceries are brought home. Taking naps in the sun . . ."

"Meow," Lutz said distinctly.

"Okay, and treats, too." Lauren put him down and got up to open the cabinet. "Liver?"

Lutz stood up, his green eyes intent on Lauren's hand.

"Liver it is," she said. Lauren tossed a treat into the air. Lutz slapped it down with his paw, and landed on it almost before it hit the floor.

"You'd make a good hockey player," Lauren said. "Too bad cats can't play hockey. Or figure skate. Or try out for school plays." She imagined Lutz dressed up as Dorothy in *The Wizard of Oz* and laughed aloud. "You *could* be the Cowardly Lion," she went on.

Lutz had finished his treat. He sat down, curled his tail neatly around his front paws, and stared hard at Lauren.

"No," she said. "No more treats." It wasn't quite time for bed. She could hear her parents' voices in the family room. It sounded as if Lacey might be in there, too. Upstairs, in the room the three sisters shared, Lisa was already asleep. She suspected that Bryan was plugged into his Walkman, with a book open in front of him, in his room.

She stretched her arms over her head and bent to touch her toes. She'd stretch and then walk through her short program for Regionals a few times before she went to sleep. When you wanted to win, there was no such thing as too much practice.

7

The ice was cold. And hard. Somehow, she always forgot how hard the ice was between falls.

Coach Perry came over to give Lauren a hand up. "Your balance is off," she said.

"I kind of noticed," Lauren said wryly.

"Concentration," Coach Perry said. "Balance is a matter of concentration. Again."

"Again," repeated Lauren. She turned and skated away from Coach Perry. Then she began the short, quick buildup to the single–double combination that opened her program. It was a dramatic opening, one designed to catch the attention not only of the judges but of her fellow competitors. The opening said, "I'm here! Watch me!"

But her fellow competitors, particularly Antonina Dubonet, who had placed a *very* close second to Lauren in their last event, would have no trouble catching Lauren if she fell at the start.

She set up, lifted her foot, spun in the air, and nailed her single. But she knew mid-spin in the double that she wasn't going to make a clean finish.

This time, she put her foot down. A two-footed landing was a bad habit to get into, but it was preferable to another body-to-ice moment so soon after the first one.

Lauren stopped. "Sorry," she said.

"Don't apologize to me," Coach Perry said. "Again."

Stifling an inward groan, Lauren made her way back down the ice. The last couple of weeks had been going so well. She'd been working so hard, practically flying through lessons and practice and even managing to squeeze in extra practice sessions. She'd basked in the sun of Coach Perry's approval. She'd enjoyed giving herself more than a few mental pats on the back.

But not today.

Today was going to be one of those bad-luck days when she wouldn't be able to do anything right. She'd just have to grit her teeth, work twice as hard, and bear it.

"You're quiet today," her mother observed as they drove back up the Northway toward Pine Creek. "Tired?"

"No," said Lauren quickly. She didn't want her mother to think skating was too much for her, ever.

She stared ahead out the window and felt, rather than saw, her quick glance toward her. After a moment she said, "I guess if you're not tired, that means you didn't try very hard in your lesson today."

"No! I killed myself!" Lauren blurted out. She stared at her mother and saw her smile.

"That's better," Mrs. Wing said.

Lauren made a sheepish face. "Okay. It was a

43

hard practice. I admit it. I spent lots of time on the ice. I mean down on the ice."

"If you're having trouble with a particular jump, you could do a different one," her mother suggested.

"No way. This is the jump combination that fits the music. And it has a higher degree of difficulty. If I can just get it right, it'll be awesome."

"Ah. The awesome factor." The corners of her mother's eyes crinkled in amusement.

"Yeah. The awesome factor," Lauren agreed. Talking about it made her feel a little better.

"Maybe if you shelved the move for a couple of days, let yourself take some time off," Mrs. Wing suggested.

"No. I don't have any time to take off," Lauren said.

"You've got time. The Regionals are close, but not *that* close," her mother said.

Lauren pulled the thermos from under the seat. "Tea?" she asked.

"Actually, it's coffee today, and I'd love some," her mother said.

Lauren poured out a cup and handed it to

her mother. Then she fished another banana out of her skate bag. She'd already eaten breakfast, but skating made her hungry. Considering her mother's suggestion, she peeled the banana and bit off a chunk.

"Regionals are too close to take *any* time off. I'll just have to work harder," Lauren said. "Besides, practice makes perfect."

"I've never known you not to work hard," her mother said. "And just remember, whatever happens, as long as you've done your best, your father and I, we'll be proud of you. Your whole family will. To us, you already are perfect."

It was a roll-your-eyes moment. But Lauren just nodded. She wasn't really listening. What good was doing your best if you didn't become the best?

No. No time off. If anything, she'd redouble her efforts.

"Check it out!" Danielle came bustling into the Pine Creek rink. She was holding the all-too-familiar blue bound copy of the script for *The Wizard of Oz*, waving it like a flag. Ever since tryouts for the play had been announced, Danielle had been taking the script everywhere with her.

"We've finished practice," Annie said. "Where were you?"

"Didn't Coach Knudson tell you? I had rehearsal." Danielle paused expectantly.

Lauren understood first. "Rehearsal? Not tryouts?"

"Those are soooo over," Danielle said.

"Then . . . oh, Danielle, did you get the part you wanted?" Lauren asked.

"You're looking at Dorothy herself," Danielle announced. She made a graceful bow. "The star of the show. Mr. Abazzia, the director, says I'm a natural. I have poise, he says."

Annie said, "That's great, Danielle! Really. But what about skating practice?"

"No worries. I'll practice after rehearsals. They're not every day. And it's only for a few weeks," Danielle told her.

"Even missing a few days of skating can set you back. I ought to know," Annie said.

"Hey, 'break a leg' is only a saying in the

theater. I'm not going to be trying to come back from an injury here, like you've had to do," Danielle said. "And it's not like I'm going to get totally out of shape. I mean, we actors have to stay healthy. People are depending on us. Mr. Abazzia says we're more than just a group of people on a stage. We're a family."

Annie and Lauren smiled at Danielle. They were like a family, too.

"Hey, Danielle," Lauren said. "Let's celebrate your getting the part and go to the Scoop Rink."

But Danielle surprised them both. "I can't," she said. She raised haughty eyebrows. "I still have to practice skating. And then I have to go home and start practicing becoming Dorothy. After all, I'm a professional. But thanks. We'll celebrate some other time, okay?" She fluttered her fingers at them. "See ya."

Annie barely waited until Danielle was gone before she said, "Danielle really has finally lost her mind."

"No, she hasn't," Lauren said. She was torn between laughing and being annoyed at Danielle.

"Huh," said Annie darkly. "You'll see. I know how hard it is stay off the ice and then try to get back on." Annie gave her thigh a thump, as if warning her foot not to try any more sneaky injuries.

"You're doing a great job," Lauren reassured her. She meant it, too. With grit and sheer determination, Annie was almost back in top form. No one would ever know that she had been injured.

"You think?" Annie said.

"I know," Lauren answered. She paused. "If Danielle's not careful, she's going to blow Regionals."

"True," Annie said.

"She's had bad luck on the ice lately," Lauren reminded Annie. "Now she gets to be a star. That's got to feel good. Maybe we shouldn't be so, you know, down on the whole idea.

Annie thought for a moment. "I guess," she said. Then she said, "I know! Maybe we could plan a sleepover or something special to celebrate Danielle's new life as a star."

Lauren glanced at Annie and Annie grinned

slyly. "Really," she said. "I'll ask my mom. And of course, while we're celebrating, we'll slip in a few hints that she should keep her eye on the ice."

"Good idea," Lauren said. Annie's house was perfect for a sleepover. She had her own room, for one thing, with twin beds *and* a trundle bed. Lauren didn't offer to have the sleepover at her house. Figuring out the arrangements for that would have been too complicated right now. Like Danielle, Lauren wanted to concentrate on a single role: becoming a champion.

8

"Sunday morning?" Mrs. Wing looked doubtfully at Lauren. "I don't know, Lauren. You don't usually practice on Sunday mornings."

"Well, maybe I should," Lauren said.

"It's Saturday and you just had a practice with Annie, didn't you?" Mrs. Wing pressed the button on the computer and the printer began to hum out pages. They were in the office above the Wings' family restaurant. Below, Lauren could hear the slamming of doors as the last of the delivery trucks dropped off supplies for the day.

"Yes. But you can't practice too much," Lauren said.

"Oh, I don't know about that." Mrs. Wing inspected the pages as they came from the printer, marking several with a red pen.

"It's just until Regionals," said Lauren. "I've got to work extra, extra hard." She didn't say, "to make up for lost time" but the words hung in the air.

Mrs. Wing looked up. "Does Coach Perry want you to practice this much?" she asked.

"Of course," said Lauren.

It wasn't exactly a lie. Coach Perry *had* said, "You need to practice transitions, especially."

She just hadn't said when. Or how much.

"I can ride my bike over. Get there early. I'll have the rink practically to myself. It'll be like private ice time. This is great!" Lauren said.

Her mother smiled. "If you say so. Meanwhile, don't we have some shopping to do? Unless, of course, you don't want a new costume for the short program?"

"Ha!" said Lauren.

Danielle stopped outside the fabric warehouse. "No place like home," she declared, borrowing a line from the movie. She brought her heels together.

"In the first place, you're not wearing ruby slippers," Lauren pointed out. "And in the second place, this is *not* home."

"We've been here so much it might as well be," Danielle said. She and Lauren followed Mrs. Wing through the glass doors of the building. Immediately, the smell of dust and fabric dye swirled up Lauren's nose.

She sneezed, then sneezed again.

"And you always sneeze when you walk in the door," Danielle added.

Then she sneezed, too.

"Gesundheit, Dorothy," Lauren said.

They moved through the patchwork quilt of aisles, brushing their fingertips along velvet, silk, cotton, and strange, unidentifiable mixtures of material. Huge bolts of material stacked to the ceiling lined the walls. Colors melted together or clashed. Plaids, checks, prints, stripes, metallic and beaded fabrics, cascades of lace, and frothy ruffles all vied for Lauren's attention.

Danielle stopped in front of a deep aquamarine velvet and cupped her face in her hands. "Blue," she declared. "I see Dorothy in blue, to represent the sky she fell out of."

"She fell out of a tornado," Lauren said. "What color is that?"

"You have *no* imagination," Danielle said.

"Some people have too much," Lauren retorted.

"There is no such thing as too much imagination," Danielle declared. "Mr. Abazzia says that imagination is the key to great theater."

Lauren sighed inwardly. She and Annie were both getting pretty tired of what Mr. Abazzia said. Aloud she said, "That is a pretty decent color blue. It'd look good out on the ice."

"Which is not *so* different from being center stage," Danielle said.

Lauren had to admit that in a way, Danielle was right.

"I'm going to ask for a sample," Danielle said.

"But wasn't Dorothy a farm girl?" Lauren reminded Danielle. "Would a kid from a farm walk around in a blue velvet dress?"

"See? NO imagination. Of course she would—*after* she got to Oz," Danielle said. She hurried off in search of a sales assistant.

Lauren smoothed the blue velvet. It was beautiful. It would make a wonderful skating outfit. But she knew without looking at the price tag that it was too expensive.

And too hot, she told herself. If you wore velvet, you'd probably melt while you were waiting to go on. With that consoling thought, she gave the velvet one last pat and wandered down the aisle.

You didn't have to wear velvet to win. You just had to be the best. If you weren't, all the velvet, silk, and satin in the world wouldn't change anything.

"A new costume is very useful," Coach Perry said at the next lesson, unwittingly echoing Lauren's thoughts. "But it will not make you a great skater. Not even talent alone will do that. You must work."

"I know," Lauren said. "Hard work and good luck."

"Champions make their own luck," Coach Perry said.

Lauren didn't answer. She was busy gulping down the juice-and-water mixture she kept in her plastic sports bottle at ringside. Cold from sitting on the ice, the liquid burned her throat. She had her opening sequence under control. But now her layback spin, normally a simple and elegant move for Lauren, was spinning out of control. The pattern her skate left on the ice looked as if she weren't spinning, but turning loops across the ice.

Dreadful, Lauren thought to herself, an expression Coach Perry used to describe unsporting conduct in skaters, coaches, or anyone else in the skating world who didn't measure up to her standards of sports etiquette.

She would never use such words to describe a skater's efforts. But Lauren used it about herself now.

Dreadful, she repeated. Regionals seemed to loom ahead, casting a shadow like an enormous tombstone.

Lauren shook off the image. There was, too,

such a thing as too much imagination, she thought. The one thing she needed now wasn't imagination, but concentration.

She set the bottle down on the ice and looked at her coach.

"Again," she said.

Rebecca inspected Lauren as she sat down next to her in class. Her sharp eyes seldom missed anything, and they didn't now. "Someone's not a happy skater," she said.

"You can say that again." Lauren sat down and thumped her book bag onto the desk. She began to jerk out books, looking for her textbook and homework.

A notebook slithered to the floor. Lauren gave it a glare that would have killed it if it had been alive.

"Allow me." Randy appeared out of nowhere and scooped up the book.

Rebecca let out a long-suffering sigh. "Randy, we don't need your help," she said. "Hand it over." She held out her hand.

"Say please," Randy teased.

"Please," said Rebecca.

"And thank you," he added.

"And thank you," she said, frowning ferociously at him.

"I don't know. You didn't sound sincere," he said.

Before she realized what she was doing, Lauren was on her feet. "Randy," she said, "Give me the notebook. RIGHT NOW!"

Randy's eyes widened in amazement. "I was just kidding, Lauren," he sputtered.

"NOW!" she said.

Randy dropped the notebook onto Lauren's desk. "Excuse me," he said.

Lauren dropped back down into her seat. What was wrong with her? One minute she'd felt blazingly angry. Now she was completely exhausted. Given half a chance, she'd probably fall into a deep sleep at her desk.

"Lauren?" Rebecca said.

"Sorry, Beck," Lauren said. "I guess I'm a little tense."

"Well, you got your notebook back," Rebecca said. "I don't know what it is with

Randy these days. I mean, he is being a total full-time pest."

"When has he ever not been?" Lauren asked.

Rebecca was watching Randy. He was trying to help his best friend Donnie balance his desk on its two back legs. Every time Donnie failed, the desk crashed down onto four legs and Randy and Donnie and all of his buddies laughed uproariously, as if it were the funniest thing they'd ever seen.

Lauren gritted her teeth. The crashing of the desk was getting on her last nerve. To her relief, the teacher walked into the classroom.

Donnie dropped his desk down with one last crash and kids began to go to their seats.

"You okay?" Rebecca asked.

"Ask me after Regionals," Lauren said. She smiled to show she was joking.

Sort of.

9

"It's going to be beautiful," Lauren breathed.

"Not if you don't stand still," her mother said. "Turn. Stop. Don't move."

Lauren stared at her reflection in the long mirror on the back of her mother's closet door. The material for her new costume for the short program was almost as elegant as the blue velvet that Danielle had finally persuaded her mother was absolutely necessary for the role of Dorothy.

Despite her mother's command to remain motionless, Lauren smoothed the soft folds of her skirt. "Was it . . . was it very expensive?" she asked. Her mother had whisked the bolt of fabric to the counter before Lauren had even had time to look at the price, then sent Lauren to look for matching thread while she'd had the material cut and priced. When Lauren returned, everything had been paid for.

Now her mother gave her head a slight shake, just as she had when Lauren had asked the same question at the fabric warehouse. "I paid what it was worth," she said.

Did that mean the fabric had been expensive? Lauren wondered. She felt a stab of guilt. Although times were not as hard as they had been for her family, the Wings still had to watch money very carefully.

Lessons cost money. Ice time cost money. Traveling to and from the lessons cost money. Entering and going to events was expensive and the more you competed, the more it cost.

Some skaters, Lauren knew, had not only coaches but choreographers and costume designers and music consultants who put together special music for their programs. And more. The better you got, the better the competition got. You could not overlook any detail if you wanted to win. Even little details cost money, too. The only thing without a price was your own effort, your own time.

"Turn. Stop. Lift your arms," her mother ordered.

Lauren obeyed automatically. She kept her eyes on herself in the mirror.

The girl with the pinned-together costume and the raised arms would be a champion some day, Lauren vowed. She'd stand at the Olympics just like this and . . .

Lauren raised her arms higher and felt the stab of a pin. "Lauren!" said her mother. "What are doing? Stand still!"

Early on a Sunday morning usually meant that the rink was almost empty, as near to private ice time as Lauren could get for practice without paying private ice rates.

But not today. Today, everyone in Pine Creek seemed to have decided that the rink was the place to be.

Who invited all the annoying people into her ice rink? Lauren glowered at the four kids scrambling by in a wild ice race. She glared at a boy and a girl who skated by, their heads close together. When a short man with a long red muffler smiled at her as he huffed and puffed past, she scowled in return.

Another couple, with a tiny girl in a ruffled skating skirt, stepped onto the rink. Each parent held her hands, pulling her along, lifting her up, and making her squeal with delight.

Lauren finished her warm-up and chose a spot far from the crowd. Gliding off her left foot, she began to count down to her opening jump sequence.

The two-footed landing from the simple single toe loop did nothing to improve her mood.

She did it again. And again. And again. But she was jinxed. She couldn't get it right. She was the bad-luck figure skater.

"Looking good," the short man said, huffing past again.

Lauren stared after him. "What do you know?" she muttered.

She went back to the edge of the rink, and started over. Again.

The phone was ringing when Lauren got home.

She answered it, dropping her skate bag with a thud. It sounded the way she had sounded all day, she thought wearily, landing on the ice on two feet, or two feet and a hand—or bottom first.

The arrival of Erica had not helped either. Lauren had felt Erica's critical, mocking eyes on her each time she fell and got up.

At least I got up, Lauren thought.

"Hello?"

"Lauren. It's me. Annie. How're you?"

"Rotten," said Lauren without thinking.

"You are?" Annie sounded surprised.

"Well, no. But I've been better. I've been at the rink all morning and I couldn't do anything right."

"Since it opened this morning? Wow. I don't think I could do that. If I didn't have at least one day off, I might crack up," Annie said.

Was Annie trying to psych her? No. Not Annie. Annie would never do that. "So what's happening?" Lauren said, trying shake off her bad mood.

"Next Friday night. What do you think?

We'll give Danielle a surprise sleepover to celebrate her getting to be Dorothy."

"Oh. Right." Lauren had almost forgotten about Danielle, whom neither she nor Annie had seen since Wednesday practice. But the time off the ice hadn't seemed to have affected Danielle's performance that much, Lauren remembered now, feeling even crankier. She was a little rusty, but she could still nail a trick. In fact, she was looking pretty confident out there on the ice.

It wasn't fair. Why did everybody else have all the luck?

"We can make a cake. An ice-cream cake. You know, the kind where you add ice cream to the cake."

"I'll bring some ice cream from the Scoop Rink," Lauren promised.

"And I'll make a salad. And we'll get veggie pizza because that's Danielle's fav. Maybe we'll even go to the movies or something. It'll be fun," Annie went on.

"Fun," Lauren said. She yawned without warning.

"Sor-ry," Annie said. "Am I boring you?"

"No! No, I just didn't get much sleep, I guess," Lauren said.

"Yeah. Tell me about it." Annie's tone changed. She lowered her voice. "I close my eyes at night and I see this big, snotty judge holding up a sign that says four-point-five."

"I keep dreaming that I get out on the ice, and I'm missing my shoelaces," Lauren confided.

"People will steal your shoelaces at competitions, you know," Annie said, her voice returning to normal. "Or fool around with your skates or your costume if you're not careful."

"Oh, Annie. No one's ever done that to you!"

"No, but I've heard about it," Annie said. She paused, then added. "But I guess if we keep an eye on Erica, we don't have *too* much to worry about."

That made Lauren laugh, and she told Annie about seeing Erica at the rink. Describing her repeated falls, and how Erica was watching, Lauren felt a little better. She hung up the phone.

She'd take a hot shower and rest her aching

feet, she decided. After all, every skater had bad practices—and as Annie had said, Erica had obviously been a jinx. What skater could fight that?

"Is that you?" Lacey zigzagged out into the hall, dribbling a small foam soccer ball.

Lauren swiped at it with her foot, sending it into the den.

"Gooooal!" Lauren said, pumping her arms in the air.

"As if," Lacey said, darting after the ball. She executed a few foot moves that almost looked like magic tricks, then looked up at Lauren with a smirk.

"Not bad," Lauren said.

"Not bad? Wait'll you see me on the field." She paused. "You haven't forgotten about the playoff game, have you?"

"I thought you'd lost your last game," Lauren said.

"Lost? Us? The Pine Creek Timberwolves? HAAAA!" Lacey flipped the ball up and caught it on her thigh, then juggled it back to her feet.

"I haven't forgotten. You win one more game and you go to the playoffs. When's the next game?"

Lacey stopped juggling and trapped the ball beneath her left foot. "You're going to come to it?"

"I might."

"Next Thursday," Lacey said.

Lauren said, "Welllll . . ."

"I know. I know. You've got practice," Lacey said. She looked disappointed and Lauren felt guilty.

"I might make it," she said, knowing she wouldn't. She could tell by Lacey's face that Lacey knew it, too.

Lacey shrugged. "Well, we'll win, whether you're there or not. We're champions."

Lauren raised her eyebrows. "The last I heard, you have to play the game before you can call yourself the winner."

"Yeah, but what do skaters know?" Lacey said.

"More than soccer players," Lauren said. "Give me the ball and I'll show you."

"Come and get it," Lacey challenged.

"You bet I will!" Lauren dropped her bag again, forgetting about her tired feet, and ran after her soccer-mad sister.

10

"Grocery shopping is *hard*," Annie declared. She fell back against the seat of the car and let out a gusty exhalation of relief.

Moira, Annie's older sister, looked amused. "All you bought was cake mix and ice cream," she said.

"And soda," Annie said. "And stuff for salad, don't forget that. Plus popcorn and bananas, in case we get hungry later."

Moira made a face. "This is the diet of champions?" she teased.

"The diet of champions at a sleepover," corrected Annie.

Lauren grinned. "Haven't you ever eaten popcorn and bananas? They're pretty good together."

"I'll take your word for it," Moira told her as they drove back to Annie's house. It was almost time for the Friday sleepover, and Lauren could tell Annie was looking forward to it.

Lauren was, too. She'd made herself quit thinking about a week of disastrous practices, and had almost managed not to think about Regionals *too* much. She hadn't yet told Annie she wanted to leave the sleepover early the next morning to practice at the Pine Creek rink. But she was sure Annie and Danielle would understand. In fact, Annie would probably want to go with her, and maybe Danielle would, too. It would be just like old times—even better if they got there early enough to have the rink mostly to themselves.

"What do you think, Lauren?" Annie asked.

They'd reached the McGraths' sturdy brick ranch house. Moira drove the car into the garage and parked it.

"What do I think about what?" Lauren asked.

She got out, and grabbed a bag of groceries from the back seat of the car. Annie did the same.

"About making the cake before Danielle comes. Then we could decorate it or something. You know, like a surprise."

"I guess so," Lauren said.

"I knew you'd agree," Annie said. They followed Moira into the house through the kitchen door that connected to the garage, and set the bags of groceries on the table.

"Good luck," said Moira. "Save me a piece— *if* it doesn't have any bananas and popcorn in it."

"Ha, ha," said Annie. "Thanks for taking us to the store."

Moira waved as she left. "No problem," she said.

"Which ice cream should I melt for the cake?" Annie asked. "Phish Food or Cherry Garcia?"

"Cherry Garcia," Lauren answered. "That's Danielle's fav."

They went to work. It was an easy cake to

make, and in less than an hour, Annie was lifting it out of the oven to cool. She looked at her watch. "In fifteen minutes, we need to turn it out of the pan onto a plate," she said.

Annie looked at her watch again, then at the wall clock over the kitchen sink. Her eyebrows drew together. "Danielle's late," she announced.

"Not very late," Lauren said. "Maybe she got stuck at rehearsal."

"She told me it wouldn't be a long one tonight," Annie said.

"Let's use your computer until she gets here," Lauren suggested.

"Good idea," said Annie. "And while we're at it, I'll just send Danielle a little e-mail to remind her where she's supposed to be right now."

But even with an e-mail, an hour passed with no sign of Danielle.

"I'm getting hungry," Annie said, switching off the computer.

"Me, too," Lauren said.

"Let's make the salad. She'll be here by the time we make that," Annie said.

But she wasn't.

Annie's expression was stormy. "Where *is* she? This is totally rude."

"We could go order the veggie pizza," Lauren suggested. "I'm hungry."

"Me, too. And too bad for Danielle. She'll just have to have hers reheated when she gets here." Annie marched to the phone. She'd just picked it up when the kitchen door burst open.

"Here I am!" Danielle sang out. She stood for a moment, posed in the doorway, almost as if she were expecting applause.

"Where *were* you?" Annie asked.

"At rehearsal," Danielle said.

"You're late," Annie said.

"What's the big deal?" Danielle said. "You haven't even gotten to the sleeping part of the sleepover yet." She smiled to show she was joking.

Annie refused to laugh. "You could have called," she said.

Danielle shrugged her pack off onto the chair. "Sorry," she said. "You know how it is."

"I do?" Annie said. Lauren could tell Annie

was about to explode. Why couldn't Danielle see how angry Annie was?

But Danielle wasn't paying any attention to Annie. She'd unzipped her pack and pulled out the script. She flipped through the pages and said, "I'm having a problem with this scene with the Scarecrow and the Tin Man. I thought you guys could help me with it. You can just read the parts aloud and then I can act my parts."

For a long moment, Annie stared at Danielle. Then she said, "Forget it, Dorothy. Right now, we're going to order pizza."

"Okay. We can do it after you order the pizza," Danielle said, still unaware of how annoying she was being.

Lauren held her breath. She was *sure* that Annie was about to go off like a rocket.

But Annie didn't. Her eyes went to the cake. She bit her lip. She took a deep breath. And she said, "Okay."

Wow, thought Lauren. What had made Annie back off? She didn't know, but she was glad that Annie and Danielle wouldn't have one of their fights.

Lauren suddenly realized that both Danielle and Annie were looking at her.

"Well?" said Danielle.

Quickly Lauren replayed the last few sentences she'd heard in her brain. Ah, yes. It was her turn to choose a topping. "Olives," she said. "Black and green."

As always, both Annie and Danielle groaned. Danielle said, "Dorothy does *not* eat olives."

"Yes, but Lauren Wing does," Lauren said. Inside, she gave a big sigh of relief. The party was going to be a success after all.

And it was.

Until Lauren rolled over in the trundle bed the next morning and looked at her watch. Half an hour until the rink opened. She had to hurry.

Trying to move like a ghost, she sat up, got her pack, and began to slip out of the room.

Annie rolled. "What's up?" she said, her voice gruff with sleep.

"I have to go," Lauren whispered. In the bed across the room, Danielle made a sound of protest and pulled the covers over her head.

"We just went to sleep," Annie protested.

Lauren's gritty eyelids told her that Annie wasn't far wrong. They'd been up almost all night, acting out the play with Danielle, adding some variations of their own. Improvisation, Danielle had called it. "A very important acting exercise," she told them solemnly.

"Like warming up to skate," Annie had said. "You do remember warming up before practice. Or a lesson. Don't you, Danielle?"

With a laugh, Danielle had said, "Silly. I'm just doing this play. I'm not giving up skating forever. Who said a person can't do lots of different things?"

"No one, I guess," Annie had admitted grudgingly.

And they'd left it at that.

Lauren had almost been able to hear Annie thinking, "It's Danielle's party. Be a good friend."

Now Annie was sitting up. "You're leaving?" she asked.

"I'm going to the rink. I want to get in an extra practice," Lauren explained.

"But we're practicing this afternoon already," Annie said.

"I know . . . you want to come with me?" Lauren offered.

"No," said Annie, abruptly. She fell back onto her pillow. "You know, there's such a thing as too much practice."

"No. I don't know that. Not the way I'm skating. I need way more practice than I'm getting," Lauren answered. She paused, waiting to see what Annie would say.

But Annie turned over, with a big, long-suffering sigh, and seemed to go back to sleep.

When Lauren got to the Pine Creek rink, she had the ice almost to herself. But even without Erica lurking like the Wicked Witch of the West, Lauren went through one of her worst practices ever.

11

"The arm! The arm!" Coach Perry rapped out.

"Oh. Right." Lauren straightened her arm so abruptly that she wobbled. She recovered and skated on.

She went through the whole last segment of her short program. When she finished, Coach Perry was staring at her, arms folded.

"What?" asked Lauren. She didn't like the way her coach was looking at her. How long had it been since she'd nailed a practice? Or for that matter, a jump?

"Come here," Coach Perry said.

"I can do it again," Lauren offered. What if

Coach Perry was about to tell Lauren that she was hopeless? That Coach Perry could do nothing to help her?

Trying to remain calm, Lauren skated over to Coach Perry. The coach stepped off the ice and sat down on the nearest bleacher. She patted the bench next to her with her bare hand. Lauren stared at her coach's silvery-pink nails.

"Lauren," Coach Perry said. "You've been working very hard."

"I have," Lauren said. "As hard as I can . . . but I can work harder. I know I can."

"I have not known you very long, but I have never yet known you not to work your hardest, do your best," her coach said. Lauren heard the faint trace of an unidentifiable accent in the coach's voice.

"But I can do better," Lauren said. "I practiced three times this weekend. I can add at least one more practice next weekend. And maybe Mom and Dad will let me go practice after dinner a couple of nights." She paused, remembering her half promise to Lacey to go to her game. Then Lauren squashed the thought and the guilt. "I mean, my parents know how important Regionals are, and I'm doing fine in school, so they . . ."

The coach held up her hand. "No," she said. "No, no." She shook her head. "No more practices. No more lessons."

"But you can't give up on me now!" Lauren burst out. Her heart was pounding as if she'd just finished a row of triples. "I'll get better. It's just a—a thing. A little bad luck. Temporary. I'll make myself do better."

But Coach Perry was shaking her head again. Lauren clenched her hands together in her lap. "Coach Perry," she said, pleadingly. She couldn't believe this was happening. It was a nightmare.

The coach put one of her own small, tanned, ungloved hands over Lauren's gloves. Lauren wondered, crazily, if the coach had painted her toenails silvery-pink too.

"I'm not giving up on you, Lauren. I'm giving you a vacation."

"I don't want a vacation!" Lauren cried.

"But you need one," her coach said. She

patted Lauren's hands, a quick, brisk pat. Then she raised her hand and swept it out, indicating the rink.

"You have been almost living on the ice, I think. When you are not on it, you think about it. Maybe you practice even at home, the moves over and over in your bedroom, in the hall, going to school."

Lauren raised her eyes to Coach Perry's face. How did Coach Perry know?

"And you go to the rink on the weekends. And each day, it feels worse. I see this."

It had felt bad, Lauren thought miserably. Not a single practice or lesson had felt right in so long. She had almost, in her most secret heart, begun to dread lacing up her skates and stepping out onto the ice.

But that was only because she'd lost her rhythm somehow. She just had to work harder. She'd get it back.

"It is too much," Coach Perry said. "You drive too hard, you drive yourself over the cliff."

"What?" said Lauren.

The coach stood up. She said, "Take off your skates."

"What?" Lauren repeated, dumbfounded.

"Take off your skates and put them in your bag. Our next lesson will be Monday. That's a week from now. Until then, I want you to ride your bike. I want you to play soccer with your sister. I want you to run in the park if you feel like it. But you must only do it if you are having fun."

"I . . . I don't understand," Lauren stammered.

Then Coach Perry said something that stunned Lauren even more. "There's more to life than skating. You have to remember that when you skate. It's the only way."

She smiled. "No skating. No practicing. Until next time, then."

"NO WAY. NO TRIPLE-FLIP WAY!" Annie cried.

Lauren took a step back. Telling Annie that Coach Perry had grounded Lauren the moment Lauren had seen Annie at school might not have been the best idea.

"Are you serious?" Annie said. "You're telling the truth?"

"Yes," Lauren said. "So I can't be at practice."

"For real," Annie said in her normal voice. She stared at Lauren. "Are you freaked?"

"Yes," said Lauren again. That was one way of putting it. Numb was another.

"Wowwww." Annie let out a long breath. "What are you going to do? How are you going to stand it?"

"I don't know," said Lauren.

"It would kill me," said Annie. "It almost did, when I hurt my foot and couldn't skate."

"I remember," Lauren said, unable to resist a little sarcasm.

Annie didn't seem to notice. "Why would she do something like that? I mean, are you actually going to do it?"

"I don't know. Maybe." Lauren had thought about it. She couldn't make up her mind.

"I gotta go," Annie said. She shook her head, and gave Lauren a sideways look. "See you later."

"Later," said Lauren.

When Annie had left, Lauren leaned against her locker, heedless of the time. What *was* she going to do?

She hadn't even told her father and mother yet. She'd just kept quiet on the long ride back from the rink that morning. Let Coach Perry explain it to them. She'd said she'd call, and Lauren knew she would.

What was she going to do?

Lauren suddenly realized that she had no idea.

Then she saw Rebecca walking toward her. "Beck," she said, with relief. "Hi."

Rebecca looked up. As usual, her red messenger bag was stuffed with books. Rebecca was leaning to one side slightly from the weight. She looked up at Lauren from beneath her bangs. "Hi," she said.

"So," said Lauren. "What're you doing this afternoon?"

12

The park was full of people. It was also, according to Rebecca, full of good smells.

"Good smells?" Lauren asked, as both Alice and Clyde, the Meyerses' two dachshunds, sniffed the bottom of a trash can with noisy enthusiasm.

Alice broke away to work on a candy wrapper next to the can.

"Oh, no you don't," Rebecca said, scooping up the wrapper and tossing it in the can. "Yes. I mean, good smells to a dog. A dog's sense of smell is about ninety bazillion times better than a human's. I mean, to Alice and Clyde, it's like our noses are blind."

"Blind," Lauren said. She sniffed. The air smelled like trees and dust from the nearby softball field.

Tugging on his leash, Clyde veered off the park path, his nose to the ground. "Whoa, Clyde," Lauren said. She had to trot to keep up.

Behind her, Rebecca said, "Don't let him pull you around like that!"

"It's his walk," Lauren answered. "He gets to choose where he wants to go."

"Okay. Come on, Alice." Rebecca and Alice followed and soon the two girls and two dogs were zigzagging all over Pine Creek Park. When they dashed across the field to arrive finally at the refreshment stand near the front gate where they'd started, Lauren burst out laughing. She bent to pet Clyde and scratch his silky ears.

"Good boy, Clyde," she told him. "Good work. But you can't have a hot dog. You *are* one."

Alice sat down next to Clyde and stared expectantly up at the man dishing out sodas and hot dogs and snacks to customers. He glanced over and smiled. "Ah," he said. "Special customers." He produced two dog biscuits and held them up.

Both dogs wagged their tails so hard that their whole bodies wriggled. But they remained seated until Rebecca said, "Okay." Then they stood up and carefully accepted a biscuit each from the hot dog vendor.

"Thank you," Rebecca said.

"Hey, my favorite customers," the man said with a smile. He turned back to take another order. Lauren and Rebecca and the dogs walked away.

"This is fun, isn't it?" Rebecca asked. "Hanging out in the park. We haven't done that in a long time."

"It is fun," Lauren admitted. She made a wry face. "But you know what? I feel like I'm playing hooky from school, or something."

"Puh-lease. Coach's orders. You're just doing what Coach Perry tells you. And I think she's pretty smart."

"You do?" Lauren asked as they left the park.

"Absolutely," Rebecca said, "I mean, it's like

studying for a test. You stare at the pages and then you start getting really, really sleepy and then you forget what you just read and you have to read it over and over, right?"

"Right."

"And then if you make yourself stay awake, you're tired the next day and maybe you don't do as well on the test as if you'd just gone to sleep," Rebecca concluded. "In fact, experiments have shown that getting a good night's sleep is just as important for test performance as studying."

"Unless you've goofed off the whole semester," Lauren said.

But Rebecca, who was in her scientist mode, said, "Of course, the study adjusted for goof-offs. But Lauren, you're not a goof-off. You're the most prepared of the prepared."

"Not lately," Lauren muttered.

"You know what you're doing," Rebecca insisted. "It's just that you're too tired to do it the best you can."

"I guess," Lauren said.

"I *know*," Rebecca said.

Clyde and Alice both turned right, up the Meyers' driveway.

"Can you stay for dinner?" Rebecca asked.

Lauren started to say no, that she had to go to bed early and she hadn't finished her homework. But then she remembered—she didn't have to go to bed early. And she and Rebecca had all ready done most of their homework that afternoon.

"Probably," she said. "I'll call home and make sure."

"Are you awake?" Lisa hissed in Lauren's ear.

"I'm awake now," Lauren said. But she smiled at her youngest sister.

She had been awake for a long time. She'd awakened in the gray light of dawn from a bad dream, one of those in which she'd studied for the wrong test and then gone to the wrong room and was late anyway.

Anxiety dreams, her mother called them.

Well, she had plenty to be anxious about—like goofing off from skating with Regionals looming. What was Coach Perry thinking? Lauren sighed.

Coach Perry was a mystery to Lauren. She didn't scare Lauren the way she first had when Lauren had started skating for her. But the coach did things her own way, no doubt about it.

This was just another one of her coaching techniques.

Yeah, thought Lauren sourly. Like, the worst yet.

"Lauren? If you're awake, why aren't you getting up?" Lisa asked.

"What are you, my alarm clock?" Lauren said. "Where's the off button?" She reached out and pretended to be searching for a ringing clock, patting Lisa on the head.

"NOOO, silly!" Lisa shrieked, forgetting to whisper.

"Some people are still trying to sleep around here," Lacey announced from the top bunk across the room. "When you win the game that sends your team to the playoffs, you should at least get some sleep."

Lisa's eyes grew wide. She held her finger to her lips. "SHHHH!" she shushed Lauren almost loud enough to be heard in the kitchen.

Lacey groaned the groan of a hibernating bear that had been rudely awakened.

"Shhh, yourself," Lauren whispered to Lisa. She swung her feet out of bed. "Let's go see what's for breakfast."

Lisa raced down the stairs ahead of Lauren, then turned expectantly. Lauren turned around and grabbed the railing. Then she bunny hopped backward to the bottom where Lisa stood. It was a skating exercise she'd made up long ago.

"What's my score?" she asked Lisa as she reached the bottom and Lisa, as always, beamed and shrieked, "SIX!"

"Six A.M., maybe," Bryan grumbled, poking his head out of the kitchen. "Could you keep it down for the people who are trying to sleep while they eat breakfast?"

"Shhh!" Lisa said to Lauren.

"That's the idea," Bryan said.

They went into the kitchen. "Hi, Mommy," Lisa said, running to fling her arms around her mother's neck.

"Morning, Lisa." Mrs. Wing gave Lisa a hug.

"Morning, Lauren. Is Lacey up?"

"Sort of," Lauren said.

She sat down and looked over at her mom. Her parents had given her the "we support your coach" talk the night before.

Now, nobody was talking about it at all—about Lauren's being there on a morning when she was supposed to be skating. It was, Lauren decided, kind of weird—as if they were afraid she might break down or something if they said anything. Was she that fanatic about skating?

"Any plans for this afternoon?" Bryan said suddenly.

Good old Bryan, Lauren thought. She smiled. "You mean, besides skating?"

"Yeah. That," he said.

Lauren poured some more o.j. "I was thinking of going over to Danielle's school. She's in a play, and I thought I'd go see her rehearse."

"Danielle? The curly blonde, right?" Bryan asked.

"Don't be a jerk, Bryan. You know who Danielle is," Lauren said.

"*I* know who Danielle is," Lisa announced.

92

"Sounds like a good idea," Mrs. Wing said, just a little too enthusiastically, in Lauren's opinion. What had Coach Perry said to them? That Lauren was about to lose it? "Treat her kindly, or she might flip out"?

"I guess," Lauren said.

"But be home for dinner," her mother said.

"I will be," Lauren said. She didn't say that she sort of hoped she could talk Danielle into going by the Pine Creek rink on the way home from rehearsal.

She'd feel funny if she didn't at least go by the rink.

After school, Lauren rode her bike to Pine Creek Academy. *The Wizard of Oz* rehearsal was fun to watch and Danielle was great. But at the end of the last scene, Lauren spotted the true Wicked Witch of the West—Erica.

"What're you doing here?" Lauren blurted out.

Erica looked almost as startled as Lauren. But she made a quick recovery. "None of your business," she said. "What are you doing here?

Aren't you supposed to be desperately practicing, in the hopes you'll get lucky at Regionals?"

"There's more to life than practicing," Lauren said. Where *was* Danielle? She'd told Lauren she'd meet her outside right away.

Raising her eyebrows in mock surprise, Erica said, "For some people, maybe. But from what I've seen of your skating lately, you need all the practice you can get."

"I'm here," Danielle interrupted them. She glanced at Erica. "And you were just leaving, right?"

Erica smiled her mean smile at Lauren. "Right," she said.

"So was I fabulous, or what?" Danielle said. "Of course, it's just rehearsal. And those are not my big scenes you saw. And the guy who's playing the Cowardly Lion? I mean, give me a break!"

"You were good," Lauren said. "Really."

That stopped Danielle. "Really?" she said.

"Triple-flip good," Lauren said, borrowing a phrase from Annie.

"Wait until you see the play," Danielle said. "I'll be even better. We all will. We just need a little more practice."

"Speaking of practice," Lauren said. "Want to go see if Annie's finished hers?"

Danielle gave Lauren a shrewd look. "If *you* want to."

Lauren thought about it. Then to her surprise, she found herself shaking her head. "No," she said. "No. Let's just hang out or something."

"Whoa!" Danielle put her hand to Lauren's forehead. "Are you feverish? Not going to the rink?"

"Am I that bad?" Lauren asked.

"That dedicated," Danielle corrected. "I figure you must be going crazy, not being able to practice. I mean, I still don't understand why Coach Perry did that."

Lauren shrugged. She hadn't figured it out either.

"*I* know," Danielle said. "It's a plot. A secret, evil plan. Coach Perry really works for a rival who wants to keep you from competing at Regionals."

95

For half a second, Lauren almost believed Danielle.

"I'm *kidding*," Danielle said. "Wow. You didn't believe I meant it, did you?"

"I don't know what I believe," Lauren said.

They walked along without speaking for a while. Then Lauren said, "Danielle, could you give up skating? Like, forever?"

"No!" said Danielle. She stopped and turned to face Lauren, planting her hands on her hips. "Are you crazy for real? Has not practicing made you go whack that fast?"

"But with the play and all, it seems as if you weren't that into skating lately," Lauren said.

"The only way I'll ever leave the ice is when they carry me off feet first," Danielle declared, flinging her arms out.

"I thought you liked being in the play. You said there was more to life than skating," Lauren said.

"There is." Suddenly Danielle was serious. "And I think being in the play has helped me on the ice. I'm calmer. I'll perform better. You'll see."

"Aren't you worried about Regionals? I mean, you haven't been at practice that much," Lauren said.

Danielle folded her hands under her chin and looked saintly. "You're not the only one who does extra practicing on her own," she said.

"When?" Lauren was surprised. "I haven't seen you when I've been there!"

"I've been going at different times," said Danielle smugly.

Lauren remembered that Danielle's family could afford to pay for ice time. "Private?"

"During the Pine Creek Figure Skating Club open rink hours," Danielle said. "I'm surprised Erica didn't tell you. She's been there, too."

"Erica and I are close, but not that close," Lauren said dryly.

"You're not?" Danielle pretended to be shocked. Then she grinned. "The play is great, though. The kids in the play are pretty cool. Not the guy who's playing the Cowardly Lion, but most of the others. And you know what? I don't miss talking about skating. It's fun talking about something else. It sort of makes skating more fun. Like, lately, it's been kind of a chore, you know. But don't tell Annie!"

Lauren realized, with a shock, that what Danielle said was true for her, too.

Somehow, recently, skating had stopped being the most fun she could have on or off the ice. Instead, lacing up her boots and stepping out onto that frozen surface had become a chore. She didn't look forward to her time in the rink, she looked forward to practice being over.

Skating had become an enemy, something she had to fight and beat.

She stopped short, amazed at the thought.

No, she was more than amazed. She was amazed and scared. What would life be like without skating? How could she even think of such a thing?

Danielle misunderstood Lauren's abrupt halt. She said, "I know, I know. I shocked you, right? Don't tell Annie. She would *so* not understand. She thinks I'm some kind of traitor for even being in this play."

Lauren still didn't say anything. She didn't

think she could be more confused, but she was.

I love skating, she told herself. I love it more than anything in the world.

But somehow, she knew that wasn't the whole truth.

"You don't think I'm a traitor, do you?" Danielle asked anxiously. For once, she wasn't being incredibly dramatic. For once, she was just being Danielle.

Lauren looked up. "Traitor? You? No. Never. Whatever you do, Danielle—well, as long as you don't rob a bank or something—I'll stick by you. That's what friends are for."

"Good," said Danielle. The frown vanished, smoothing her forehead. She grinned. "I guess that means I have to hold off on the holdup, huh?"

"I guess. And anyway, those photographs on the wanted posters at the post office are *not* star quality," Lauren said.

Danielle laughed.

Lauren only managed a weak smile.

Inside, she was wondering if her life as a

skater was about to come to an end. Was that what Coach Perry was trying to tell her? Was that why she suddenly was skating so badly?

Had her luck run out? Were her skating dreams about to melt away forever?

13

"YEAH, LACEY! HEY, LACEY! WE'RE OVER HERE!" Lisa leaned over, waving her arms, and Lauren grabbed her by the back of her T-shirt to haul her upright.

"Careful," she said. "No diving out of the bleachers."

Lisa didn't hear her. She kept windmilling her arms and calling Lacey's name.

Lacey's team did a final cheer before the second half began. Then she waved at her fans in the stands: the whole Wing family.

Even me, thought Lauren.

It was a gray, damp Saturday morning. On

any other Saturday, Lauren would have been at the rink.

But this was the playoff game: the Pine Creek Timberwolves versus the Mountain Academy Bears.

Lauren had promised to be there. But deep in her heart, she knew she might not have been—*if* Coach Perry had not grounded her.

And that would have been wrong. The joy in Lacey's face when Lauren had said she'd be at the game that morning with the rest of the family had told Lauren just how wrong it would have been.

The teams trotted back out onto the field. They lined up, looking small and fierce in their big shirts and bulky shinguards.

Lacey danced in place at left midfield.

"That's it," Bryan said. "Stay on your toes, Lacey."

The ref blew her whistle and the second half began.

Suddenly everything was in motion at once. The ball sailed up and down the field. It zigzagged in and out among what seemed like hundreds of thrusting, kicking feet.

A Bear launched a shot dangerously close to the Timberwolf goal and Lauren found herself on her feet screaming "NOOOO!"

The goalie fell on the ball. A Bear forward fell on the goalie. A Timberwolf fullback fell on them both.

The ref blew the whistle. The goalie settled the ball and kicked it back into play.

Up and down the field they went. The score was tied 0–0 and Lauren clenched her fists. What was taking them so long! They had to score! Soon. Time was running out.

Then Lacey broke through. Her hand went up. Far across the field the right wing looked up and saw Lacey. Somehow, she managed to slide the two Bear defenders who were guarding her. One player turned as if she was going to chase the pass.

Lacey pounced on it and raced ahead.

Now the right wing was racing too, angling toward the goal, staying even with Lacey.

"SHOOOT!" Lauren screamed.

Beside her Lisa was shouting, "LACEY, LACEY, LACEY!" as Mrs. Wing held her up to see. Bryan was pounding on his father's shoulder, and Mr. Wing was shouting, too.

The goalie made a move toward Lacey.

Lacey tapped the ball with the side of her foot, a short, quick pass to the dead center front of the goal.

And the Timberwolf wing was on it, poking it into the back of the net, just past the agonized goalie's outstretched hands.

Lauren let out a whoop that rattled her brain as the team swarmed upfield to scoop up their champions.

The Bears fought hard after that, but they didn't get the goal back. The game ended Timberwolves 1, Bears 0.

"YOU WON!" Lisa shouted and threw her arms around Lacey as she came toward them after the final cheer for the other team.

"We did. Your cheering helped lots," Lacey said. She sat down to take off her cleats and put on her sneakers. "Great game," Lauren said. And it was. She hadn't seen her sister play soccer in a long time. Lacey had gotten good. Very good.

When had that happened?

"Yep," said Lacey, trying to be casual.

"Perfect pass," Bryan said. "I couldn't have done it better myself."

"Not unless you had a hockey stick," Lacey retorted.

Mr. Wing laughed. "Way to play," he told Lacey. "You're a champ."

"And a great team player," Mrs. Wing said.

Lacey was blushing. She said, "Team comes first." She finished knotting her sneaker laces. Then she leaped to her feet. "WE WON!" she shouted, scooping Lisa up.

Lisa wriggled free. "You look like you took a bath in dirt," she said.

"I almost did," Lacey said. She grinned, looking very much like Bryan when she did. "It's the price of being a star."

Normally, Lauren would probably have taken the chance to point out that skating was a much cleaner sport. But not today. She didn't want to talk about skating. It was bad enough that she'd been thinking about it practically nonstop all week.

Lacey said, "I'm glad you guys could make it. It was nice having a private cheering section."

"Me, too," Lauren said.

"Really," said Lacey. She gave Lauren a knowing look. "You wouldn't rather be skating?"

Lauren thought about it. She looked at her soccer star, team player, assist-making sister. Practically the only part of Lacey that wasn't covered in dirt was her teeth.

"No," said Lauren, and meant it. "No, I'd rather be here. With the champ."

Lacey ducked her head, looking almost shy. Then she looked up again. "Let's go home so I can get ready for the team party tonight," she said.

As they walked away from the soccer field, Lauren thought, This is what other people do. This is what people do all the time. Homework. Soccer. Plays. Hanging out with their friends.

Most people didn't spend most of their time in a big cold rink skating, jumping, spinning— and crashing—across the ice.

She looked back at the soccer field.

"Are you going to play soccer at the party?" Lisa asked, sliding her hand into Lacey's.

"You bet," Lacey told her. "I'd play soccer all day every day if I could."

"Would you?" Lauren asked.

"Naturally." Lacey gave Lauren a sideways glance. "Same as you do skating," she said. "You know, it's like, when you're doing it, you don't think about anything else. Just the love of the game."

Or the ice, thought Lauren. And for the first time in a long time felt a rush of excitement when she thought about skating.

She threw one arm around Lacey's shoulders and gave her a hug of happiness.

Lacey pulled back. "Hey," she complained. "Watch it! You're rubbing off the dirt!"

The Silver Springs rink hadn't changed. It was still big, and almost new, and shiny and cold. When Lauren came out of the locker room on Monday morning, Coach Perry in her familiar taxi-yellow parka was sitting at the far end in her usual place as if she had never left at all.

"Good morning," she said.

"It's a great morning," Lauren said. She took a deep breath of cold air. It smelled like ice, the ice in a skating rink. It was a smell Lauren could recognize in her sleep.

It was, thought Lauren rapturously, a beautiful smell.

She took another deep breath.

The coach took a tiny sip of hot chocolate. "So. Did you have a good vacation from skating?"

"Yes," said Lauren and was surprised to realize that the answer was more or less the truth.

"Do you know why I told you to take a vacation?" the coach continued.

Lauren slid her skate bag onto the floor next to the rink's edge. She sat down next to Coach Perry to remove her skate guards and pull on her gloves.

"Yes," she said. "I think I do."

Coach Perry raised her eyebrows in a question.

"Because all I could think about was winning. Winning is important, but not if you don't care about what you're doing," Lauren said softly.

Her coach nodded.

Lauren went on, "I—my whole family—we've given up a lot for skating. I guess I don't lead such an ordinary life. Other kids hang out. You know. They're soccer players or in school plays. They do homework together. Go to camp.

"I don't. I don't even do things with my family all that much. Because of skating. But it's what I want to do. It's what I'm best at in the world. It's what I love," Lauren looked up at her coach. "And I know it's not bad luck or good luck that decides how I do. It's me."

"A very good vacation, then," Coach Perry said. She set down her cup and stood up.

Lauren stood up, too. She stepped out onto the ice and turned to face her coach. She grinned and took another deep breath of icy air. Soon, her breathing would be short and hard. Soon, her legs would be burning and her arms would feel like lead. And soon, somewhere in the middle of all that, she'd fly across the ice for a few moments as if she was weightless, soar above it as if she never had to come back down.

She could hardly wait.

14

The phone rang and woke Lauren from her sleep. She put the phone to her ear and mumbled a hello.

"Mrrrowww."

It was a familiar early morning sound, but not over the telephone.

Lauren rubbed at her eyes and stared at the phone receiver in her hand.

"MrrrrOWW!" she heard.

Then a louder, "Ouch!"

Lacey's voice, tiny and far away, saying, "I told you not to squeeze Lutz, Lisa. He doesn't like it."

"He scratched me," Lisa cried.

"He should have. You shouldn't have squeezed him."

"But I wanted him to say good morning to Lauren," Lisa said.

Lauren blinked, as she heard her older brother Bryan's voice, saying, "Give me the phone."

"Lauren? Can you hear me?" Bryan asked.

Lauren started to laugh as she held the phone up to her ear. "Yes," she said. "Loud and clear."

"We called to wish you luck," said Bryan. "And don't worry. You can stop any shot they throw at you."

Bryan the hockey freak, Lauren thought. "Got it," she said. "Thanks."

"Here's Lisa and Lacey," Bryan said. "Tell Mom hello."

"She's in the shower," Lauren answered. "I'll tell her. . . ."

"Lauren!" Lisa shouted. She loved talking on the phone—the louder, the better.

"Don't shout, Lisa," Lacey said.

"Lutz said hello, too, but then he scratched

112

me," Lisa went on, lowering her voice only slightly.

"Did you scratch him first?" Lauren teased her sister.

"No!" Lisa shouted.

"It's my turn," Lacey said.

"Good-bye," Lisa said. "Good luck!"

"No! Don't hang up," Lauren heard Lacey say. There was a clunking sound, as if the phone had been dropped, then Lacey said, "Hey, Lauren."

"Hi. How's it going?"

Lacey snorted. "Dad already left for work, and Bryan thinks he's in charge."

"Sounds horrible."

"Yeah. I wish you were going to be on television. Then we could watch."

"I don't know if that's what I'd wish. I'm nervous enough as it is," Lauren said.

"You'll get used to it," Lacey said. She paused. Lauren heard her say something. Then Lacey said, "Bryan says I have to get off the phone. Tell Mom hi. And skate great."

"I'll try," Lauren said. Suddenly, she was

barely able to speak for the lump in her throat. How was it possible that she was homesick? She'd been gone only a couple of days.

"'Bye," Lacey said.

"'Bye," Lauren whispered as the line went dead.

"Was that the phone?" Lauren's mother asked as she emerged from the bathroom, toweling her hair dry.

"Yep." Lauren made her tone cheerful. "Bryan and Lacey and Lisa send their love. They called to wish me luck."

"The Lauren Wing fan club," Mrs. Wing said. "Smarter *and* better-looking than your average fan club."

Lauren laughed at that. "Yeah, right," she said. She headed for the shower, but first stopped to admire the huge banner that Rebecca had made on the computer. "Good Luck, Lauren," it read. Lauren bit her lip. She knew that she would need more than luck at today's Regional Championship.

* * *

Too big, Lauren thought in a daze.

Way too big.

Lauren gripped the railing of the skating rink. This arena was huge.

In a very short time, she, Lauren Wing, ten going on eleven, would be skating in the Regionals, in front of the biggest audience of her life. It made her feel small. And alone.

So what? she asked herself. No matter how many people are in the stands, it doesn't change the ice.

And you know the ice.

Cold.

Lauren smiled a little at her joke. She felt slightly better. But she decided she didn't want to look at all those empty seats anymore and imagine them filled with people—people she didn't know.

Abruptly she turned and headed back to the locker room to get ready for her practice session. As Lauren made her way to the locker she'd claimed in the back corner, skaters brushed by her, laughing and talking. They carried enormous skating bags full of gear, smaller bags with skates inside, coat hangers with plastic bags encasing glittering costumes, hanging bags bulging with clothes.

Most of the skaters were older than Lauren. All of them seemed to her much more sophisticated and sure of themselves, as if competing in Regionals were just another day at the rink.

But at least she would be just as fashionable as the rest of the skating crowd, Lauren thought. She stopped for a second to admire herself in a locker room mirror, grateful all over again to her best friends for their help.

She had borrowed the pink wrap skirt that she wore over her long-sleeved black leotard from Annie. Annie was responsible, too, for the matching pink legwarmers over the black tights.

Annie and Danielle (who would both be practicing later) had both had a hand in Lauren's fashion prep. Lauren smiled and smoothed the skirt, remembering the "fashion practice" Annie had called at her house one afternoon after their rink time together. Annie had flung clothes out of her closet so fast that Danielle and Lauren hadn't been able to catch them all.

"You know the judges are watching, even when you practice," Annie had said, backing out of the closet to hold up a white sweater woven with metallic thread. "You have to look pulled together at *all* times. It's like, quintuple-toe-loop important."

"Quintuple-toe-loop?" Lauren had said, trying not to laugh at this even more exaggerated turn of phrase than usual from Annie.

Danielle had removed the sweater from Annie's hand and restored it to the hanger. "Not in glitter," she declared. "Not at practice. You'll look like you're trying too hard. And go easy on the practice makeup, too."

"No glitter? You?" Annie had glanced over her shoulder in fake surprise.

"Having a sense of drama doesn't mean *tacky*," Danielle had said, loftily.

Not only had Lauren come away with the matching legwarmers and skirt, but Danielle had contributed another pair of legwarmers with matching gloves and headband.

Thanks to them, Lauren looked pulled together for the practice session on the rink. She shouldn't feel so alone.

"Lauren." It was Coach Eve Perry's voice. She was peering down the row of lockers.

"I'll be right there," said Lauren.

Lauren hoisted her skate bag and headed for the ice.

Even in a rink as big as this one, Coach Perry was easy to find in her yellow coat. Although she had shoved her hands deep into the pockets of the coat, Lauren knew that her coach wouldn't be wearing gloves and that she would be wearing nail polish.

Nor was Lauren surprised when Coach Perry said, without preamble, "Basics first."

Even at Regionals, some things never changed.

Lauren finished lacing her skates as the coach went over her practice instructions. Then she removed her skate guards, smiled at Coach Perry, and stepped out onto the ice trying to look confident and calm.

Slowly, concentrating on her form and on relaxing her muscles, Lauren skated the perimeter of the rink. She pretended she didn't notice the other skaters zooming around the ice with her, but she watched them out of the corner of her eye. She spotted Antonina Dubonet, who had beaten her at another competition. Like Lauren, Antonina looked as if she'd stepped off the pages of a fashion magazine for skaters, with a flowered skating skirt that complemented the sky blue of her leotard and tights.

Another skater, a small wiry girl, was wearing a green unitard and a fuzzy white sweater. Her long braid had been threaded with fuzzy white yarn before it had been wound into a coronet around her head.

"Stop it," Coach Perry commanded as Lauren returned to the ringside where her coach stood.

"What?" Lauren said.

"Looking at the other skaters. Leave that to the spectators," Coach Perry said. She waved her hand dismissively.

The spectators, Lauren thought. What

spectators? Then she realized that quite a few people now dotted the stands, some alone, some in small groups. Several had notebooks and a few had laptops. Were these judges? Or the coaches of other skaters? Parents?

Lauren had asked her mother not to watch the practice session. Without her mother there, Lauren could focus on Coach Perry.

"Just be there for my programs," she'd said, and her mother had understood.

But some parents, Lauren knew, came to every practice, even participated and commented on what the coach was doing. Lauren was glad her parents weren't like that.

"And stop looking at the spectators," Coach Perry went on, interrupting Lauren's thoughts. "It doesn't matter who they are."

Lauren sighed. Coach Perry was right—even if the number of spectators at this practice session was larger than the number of spectators at many of the skating events Lauren had attended up until now. No matter who they were, or how many, they didn't matter.

What mattered was having a good practice.

She pushed off, allowing herself to glance at the other skaters only to make sure that she didn't get in the way of anyone setting up for a jump, and to indicate which way she was going to pass.

The girl in the green unitard nailed three jumps in a row, and threw back her head to stare challengingly up into the stands.

A man high in the bleachers broke into applause.

An overzealous coach? An overenthusiastic parent?

No one else glanced at the clapping man, and he soon stopped.

Another set of music went on, giving the skater whose performance piece it was the automatic right of way on the ice.

Now Antonina was doing back crossovers to set up for her jump. One, two, she snapped through them, getting impressive height.

Higher than me, Lauren thought, and then stopped herself. No, she thought. It's not what's important. It doesn't matter.

Today she would practice her hardest.

Tomorrow she would compete her best. No, better than her best, as Coach Perry always said.

And that was all that mattered.

15

"You're next," said the judge, touching Lauren's shoulder.

Lauren looked up. "Now?" she said. Her voice squeaked.

The judge nodded and gave Lauren an encouraging smile.

Coach Perry said, softly, "Better than your best."

It was what Coach Perry said over and over again in practice. It was what she had said before Lauren had skated her short program, what she always said.

The familiar words calmed Lauren. Suddenly, more than anything else in the world, she wanted to win. After her short program she was in second place. She knew that Antonina Dubonet had performed more confidently. Antonina was, as she had been at the previous competiton, the one to beat.

But Lauren knew Annie was struggling. The long time off the ice with the injury had cost her in subtle ways that only a judge's critical eye could detect.

But Annie hadn't given up. And now she was whispering to Lauren, "Kick ice."

Somewhere, in the locker room behind her, Danielle was in line for the bathroom. But Lauren knew she'd be there any moment to cheer her on.

Just as she had cheered Annie and Danielle on.

Lauren smiled, nodded, squeezed Annie's hand.

I am not afraid, she told herself. Suddenly it was true. She wanted to skate more than anything else in the world.

Stepping into the rink, Lauren looked neither left nor right as she skated to center ice. She raised her arms, and the music began.

Lauren held her pose for a long moment. She lowered her arm slowly. Then, with an easy, swooping glide, as if she had all the time in the world, she began her short program.

Double toe loop, double Axel. Yes. She got it. Layback spin into a spread eagle. She concentrated on keeping her body line long and elegant.

She felt the ice beneath her blades, remembered thinking that she was *almost* too close to the wall of the rink.

And then the only thing she had left to do was to end her final spin at the same moment the music stopped.

Was she a blur of motion to the judges? She hoped so. She couldn't spin for three minutes and twenty seconds, the longest spin on record, nor could she manage 240 rotations a minute, another record.

But she could try.

She didn't feel as if she was moving at all. She felt as if she were the center of a hurricane, with all the world spinning around her. The competition had gone so fast.

Until there she was, finishing her program.

She stopped and lifted her arms triumphantly, breathlessly, exactly on the last note of the music.

The crowd cheered and some of them got to their feet.

The wave of sound surprised her. She'd forgotten that so many people filled the stands.

Then she realized they were cheering for her—and for the perfect program she had just skated.

Exhilarated, she almost sprinted off the ice to where Coach Perry waited.

"Very nice," Coach Perry said. "Very nice indeed."

These were words of strong praise from her coach. Lauren grinned. "It wasn't bad, was it?" she asked.

Coach Perry's eyebrows went up, but she smiled back.

Antonina still had to skate. But she would have to skate very, very well indeed to stay in first place.

Lauren's eyes swept the stands. She found

her mother and grinned broadly. Her mother, usually so calm, was standing, holding her hands above her head to applaud.

As if Mrs. Wing was leading the cheering section, the whole crowd began to applaud, too.

Lauren saw her scores.

Her mouth dropped open. "Triple, triple back flip," she breathed.

And then her second set of marks went up for artistry and Lauren sat down hard on the nearest chair. She had received the highest scores.

"Congratulations," the judge said, smiling at Lauren.

"Thank you," said Lauren. She lowered her head slightly. As the ribbon with the gold medal on it slipped around her neck, she felt the medal press against her chest.

Her heart.

On one side of her stood Antonina Dubonet, who had won second. She had skated well, but a little too carefully. On the other side stood Annie. She'd fought through to win third.

Danielle had managed to edge Erica out for fourth. After her rave reviews as Dorothy in the play and a program she loved, Danielle was very happy. No medal. But she was standing on the sidelines, applauding. They'd made it this far. All of them. Skater's luck.

Champion's luck.

Beside Danielle, the small, wiry girl whose name was Crystal Adams was gripping the edge of the rink, just staring.

Crystal had wobbled and touched the ice once in her long program. It was a little mistake, but at this level of competition, even little mistakes could hurt you badly. Still, she had been good enough, even so, to tie with Erica at fifth place.

Erica wasn't fighting back tears. Her arms were folded and she was glaring. No way Erica would ever applaud for anyone but herself.

Lauren put one hand up and let her fingers close over the smooth, cold surface of the medal. She raised her other hand to wave at the crowd as people applauded.

It was a dream—an amazing dream come true.

"Congratulations," a tall boy said as Lauren carried her gear bag toward the Wings' battered Subaru.

"Thank you," said Lauren.

"Good work. Congratulations," another older man said. Lauren recognized him as one of the coaches.

"Thank you," she said again.

"Hey, Lauren, see you at Sectionals." Lauren turned to see Antonina Dubonet loading her gear bag into a nearby car in the parking lot of the rink. It was late. Most of the spectators had left and parking lot lights were flickering on.

"I guess so," Lauren said. "Congratulations again, Antonina."

"You, too. And call me Nina. Everybody does." Nina flashed a megawatt smile. "So when I beat you at Sectionals, you can say, 'Congratulations, Nina.'"

Lauren laughed aloud. Nina laughed, too. Lauren said, "I guess this could be the beginning of a world-class rivalry."

"World-class," said Nina. "I like the sound of that."

She waved and climbed into the car.

Lauren turned, stopped, and frowned. The headlights of a car making its way slowly out of the parking lot had spotlighted someone else Lauren knew. It was Crystal.

But this wasn't the exuberant jumping bean who'd performed so well on the ice, who'd only made one mistake and had still, with that mistake, earned fifth.

This was a slight, hunched-over figure, her head bowed, her arms folded. Towering over her was a man who Lauren was pretty sure was a coach.

And although they were a long way away, Lauren was pretty certain, too, from his gestures and the way Crystal was standing, that the man was yelling at Crystal.

What kind of coach was that? Lauren's frown deepened.

Then someone said, "Good luck at Sectionals, Lauren," and Lauren looked away to see a girl of about seven or eight whom she didn't know. Lauren searched her brain for a name. Was this girl one of the very young skaters? Did Lauren know her?

"Uh, thanks," said Lauren as the girl passed her.

Almost immediately, two other people congratulated her, using her name. Only then did Lauren realize that she wasn't supposed to know any of them. They had seen her skate. They knew who *she* was.

They were, in a way, fans.

Wow, thought Lauren. Wait until I tell my family and Rebecca.

"Lauren!" It was Annie. She jogged up to Lauren and threw her arms around her. "Pine Creek skaters kick ice," she said.

Lauren hugged Annie back. "If it hadn't been for your messed-up foot," she said.

Annie stopped her. "No excuses," she said. "And don't worry. I'll be back . . . see you at practice Monday."

Turning, Annie hustled across the parking lot to where her family waited.

Danielle had already left, making a suitably

dramatic exit, hanging out the window, shouting and cheering all the way out of the parking lot.

Lauren walked toward her mother's car and looked back at the ice arena.

I'm going to Sectionals, she thought.

And then, unable to stop herself, Lauren Wing leaped into the air in a jump that would have made Coach Perry faint in horror as she let out a whoop of joy.

Ask Michelle!

If you have a question that you would like to ask Michelle, visit http://www.skatingdreams.com

Who are some of your role models outside of skating?

My biggest role models have always been my parents. They've always been there for me and for my family and for each other. I've never known two people who worked harder, but they've never made their hard work seem, well, *hard*. The reason is that they do it out of love.

My parents are honest with me and keep me focused on the things that really count. To them it's more important that I'm *enjoying* my skating than that I'm winning my competitions. They taught me how to have respect, discipline, and loyalty. They were also the ones who first told me, "Work hard, be yourself, and have fun." I still think that's some of the best advice I've ever gotten.

How do you psych yourself before a competition?

That's a very good question. It's important to be in the right frame of mind before you skate, because so much is riding on those few minutes. I don't psych myself up in the sense of getting really excited. Instead,

I try to get calm and focused. I visualize exactly what I want to do on the ice. I just try to relax into the moment. I say to myself, "Here I am in this huge arena, with all these people waiting to see me skate. It's what all my hard work has been for. Now just go out and enjoy it."

How long does it take you to learn a difficult new move?

A day. A month. A year. It all depends on the move. It all depends on how well your body type and style are suited to the move. I succeeded in doing a triple Lutz the very first time I tried it! But then in a couple of important competitions, it was the Lutz that tripped me up. So the truth is, you're *never* done learning a move. No matter how quickly you get it, you still have to work on it, practice it, perfect it, over and over. It never ends.

Is it hard to do a triple-flip jump in your short program?

The triple flip is one of the hardest jumps to do, but all triple jumps are difficult. In general, it's true, however, that the short program can be more nerve-racking than the long program. In the short program, you have to hit every required element perfectly. The slightest mistake will show in your score. There's far less room for error than in the long program, where artistry counts for as much as technical perfection.

Don't you get dizzy when you are spinning?

At first, I did. I fell down after trying it the first few times! But you learn to focus on a single spot. You try to keep your mind and vision still and let your body do the spinning. It's something you get used to, after a while. Still, you may notice that skaters usually put their fastest spin—the toplike "scratch spin"—at the very end of their program.